Contents.

Introduction.

I first realised I really enjoyed writing
when I was at Junior School, taking great
pleasure in the creation of pieces of
written work and enjoying the occasional
praise of my teachers. Even when school
was no longer a pleasurable place, writing
was still a source of gratification and,
increasingly, catharsis. Although, I write
in many forms, it is poetry which I am
most drawn to and which I find easiest to
write. I have continued to write
throughout my life but often life was too
busy, too interesting or too hazy to do
more than write in bursts before moving on
to new activities and experiences.
Nevertheless, all those experiences were
retained and analysed and would often
emerge in a surge of creative outpouring.
A combination of events has conspired
together to allow me the time to revisit,
re-appraise and edit the poems that
document the decades of my life.

Those and other poems are recreated here,
a record of the experiences of one
ordinary person for whom the written
word was, both, a means of recording the
meanings of a life and an escape into the
realm of imagination and fantasy. Sadly,
what aren' t here are all those poems I
wrote in my head and didn' t commit to
paper or those I created when I awoke in
the night with fully formed verses clear
in my mind but which were unremembered by
the morning. Some of those poems were
truly stupendous!

Section 1

As a child living in a country village in the 1950's and 60's it was second nature to spend as much time as possible in the countryside absorbing, without conscious acknowledgement, its constantly evolving beauty and everyday variations, as well as its harshness and cruelty. Hour after hour would be spent absorbing how country life ebbed and flowed, as each day passed from morning through to night. The flow of the months and the seasons were all mapped subconsciously, as my friends and I ran, walked or climbed our way through the countryside, scaling the cliffs, or the haystacks, before leaping fearlessly into the childish unknown, or else trying to sneak, Native American Indian style, carefully through the tall grass or wheat, hopefully traversing the field whilst leaving no visible track. It may have taken us an hour to cross one field but in the process we learnt patience and how to interact with nature whilst doing minimal harm in the process. In those moments of time we could perceive nature, learn its moods and its tides, sense its balance and appreciate its peace and violence.

In later years, as I grew older, the countryside took on a different aspect, the pace more sedate but the understanding more complex and more compelling, becoming a place of experience, of reflection; by turns, a place of solitude and sociability. Walks alone, particularly at night with the stars bright and endless, were permeated by thoughts as seemingly endless and vast as the universe. Walks with others were times of discussion and observation of nature and the world, as well as time for silent companionship. At other times, the senses were simply overwhelmed by the variety and urgency of the countryside. Throughout all this and unrecognised, the poetry of the countryside became infused into my mind, and the flow of the countryside became the flow of my thoughts as I walked the paths of my experiences.

Evocation.

Barely noticed murmur of the river passing by,
loud, raucous note in the seagull's cry,
breeze in the grass, a whispering sigh,
rustling leaves as my feet pass by.

Cold, brown soil in a winter flower bed,
a walk along paths unconsciously decided,
memories of things I once desired,
that now, like summer flowers,
have long expired.

Skeletal trees, barren, bare,
cold clings to my bones as I stand and stare
at the land all about, the way that it fares,
in this wintry season of nature's affairs.

Brush through a fog that softens the land,
droplets of mist on my hair and my hand,
pacing the riverside, footsteps in sand,
all is muted in this shadow land.

Frost licks the country, all seems still,
treading a white path, wherever I will,
breathe in the cold air, taking my fill,
visions of past times, here, on this hill.

The river, quiet, murmurs at night,
my feet, restless with memories bright,
return, yet again, in the dim half-light,
to wander, as vagabond thoughts,
the paths of night.

Feeling akin to the river, the trees,
solaced once more by the touch of a breeze,
memories thought forgotten
with unconscious ease,
now consciously remembered in solitary reprise.

Night-time is fallen, shadowed, dim,
I follow old paths, melancholy within,
moon risen early, pale, thin,
I fashion one more verse to remember you in.

I'd wander forever these paths if I could,
this patch of country is deep in my blood,
every blade of grass, each branch in the wood,
creates the illusion of how still time stood.

Celebration.

Into the dripping boughs silence
pattered the self-absorbed rain;
hollow-eyed moonlight
cratered a shadowed terrain;
the air in wetness glistened,
dancing in crystal refrain.

Mossed, green features wakened
to the threnody in the air;
into the dipping boughs silence
crystalline eyes turned to stare
and the wind held, gripped in stasis,
the image forming there.

Among sallow-eyed silhouettes,
within the livening limbs,
aged, atrophied senses stir
as, dew bedecked disciples,
within Spring's greenery
whisper,

'The ritual begins'.

Tumultuous silence echoing,
'It's near, near, so near'.
A voice, star-filled, sings,
compelling all to hear,
starlit beauty crystallised,

oh, so perilously clear.
Amid a timeless, shimmering mist,
a Dryad dancing free,
each movement a perfect match
of what was,
or what will be.
At each footfall a flower springs,
fashioned from her memory.

A sylvan breeze in gentle sway
echoes the Dryad's sound,
dew spilt in rainbow light,
from flowers,
to the ground,
grasped in reflected light
the spider's webbing found.
Collected images,
diffused and grey,
clouds consume the light;
Dryad form dissolves away
before their dying sight;
space strewn stars once more concealed
bring back the crow-black night.

Into the dripping, boughs silence,
pattered the now absorbed rain;
when the black, crow night
darkened the terrain;
the wind in sylvan memory
echoed a Dryad's refrain.

Seasonal Variations.

Summer rolled by and surprised Autumn,
sleeping gently beneath a hedgerow.
Autumn awoke slowly, rearranged her leaves
and yawned.
Summer simmered and moaned she didn't get
nearly enough time,
before wandering off,
looking for a drink.

Autumn faded slowly
and gloriously away,
to be succeeded by Winter,
sneaking up with cool precision.

Winter and Spring held combat on the
Annual Plain
before Spring concluded a lingering win.

And so, in due time, back came Summer,
her long days and short nights
quietly blossoming and desperately trying
not to awaken Autumn.

Section 2.

The 1960's was a strange decade, filled with both hope and despair. Like so many who lived through the sixties, The Cold War, The Cuban Missile Crisis of 1962, which occurred not long after my ninth birthday, the Vietnam War and other such global events had a profound effect upon our psyches as nightmare scenes often infiltrated the imagination, dreams were often disturbed by vivid images of bombs, missiles and death falling from the sky. In those times many people felt lost and beheld a future that was no future. It's no surprise, therefore, that such images also became committed to paper. My first ever poem, 'Dead', written when I was fourteen, was inspired, if that is the right word, by these alarming events and it expressed the sense of hopelessness and bewilderment that I, and many of the young people I knew, felt at the time.

Dead.

The Bomb has fallen.
Destruction everywhere,
chaos everywhere,
death everywhere.
I stand alone,

no-one else is here,
nobody left.
Everyone dead,
dead,
but not me.
Why me?
Why aren't I dead?
Why should I live?

Everywhere is silent.
No birds, no cars,
no people.
No people, only me.
What can I do?
What's the use?

Listen,
do I hear voices; cars; birds.
Is this madness?
Does it matter?
How long can I last?
How long will I live?

I should end it now
before I do go mad.

No.
There may be others
I survived,

others may have, too.
Why not?
But there are no others.
The Bomb has won.

Let it stay that way.

Into Pain-Crazed Insanity They Pass.

Sallow sun sinking slowly down,
dislocated darkness presses round,
the barely noticed, sighing sound
of the scarcely breathing, dying town.
Empty headed people cry,
as their red-rimmed, tearful, bloodshot eyes,
barely notice the empty, darkening sky,
or the dying bird's forsaken sigh.

Those fun loving people seeking mirth
from careless youth of thoughtless birth,
learn ignorance of little worth
against destruction of defenceless Earth.
Mind-blown junkies taking hash,
scarcely hear the howling wind-gusts lash
and prematurely uproot their essential grass,
as into pain-crazed insanity they pass.

Cobalt Moon, suspicious light,
illumes afresh the pain-filled night;
mirth-ravaged faces, bathed in fright,
await, time conscious, their noose pulled tight.
Faded, dipped beams of abandoned cars,
like far off pinpricks of clustered stars,
cannot outshine the neon lit, crumbling bars,
where crumbling people lament to crumbling
guitars.

Section 3.

Obviously, the world did not end and even though the darkness and dread sometimes returned, people returned to what could be called 'the normal routine of life'. It was also the time when the ideology of the Hippies emerged to challenge prevailing social norms, ideas which I found very appealing. Young people met, talked, fell in love, fell out of love, had understandings as well as misunderstandings, did good things and bad things to one another as we tried to adjust to the new values and ideas. I was no exception as the following explore.

Time Will Tell.

Time will tell
if love shall sell
and not be given freely;
if so,
then I shall sell
my love
for nought,
or,
to the highest bidder.

Passing Fancies.

Where do I begin
to apologise for all the things
I did,
but not knowing what I was doing?
You, who bore the brunt,
you, who stood out front,
as I passed,
often oblivious
of the direction I was taking.
I never realised
that the reflections from the lights
mostly hid that which I had thought to see.
The truths I sought to know,
were only there for show,
and I rarely learnt what truth was meant to be.
All you who passed in line,
who believed in me for a time,
deserved better answer than I gave
when you began
to ask me 'Why?
and the reasons for the lies
that I told you
in an uncertain bid
to hold back the rising tide,
of when you grew unsure

of the emotions that I wore
as a suit of armour
to protect me from the world.
You misinterpreted the signs
as this actor spoke his lines
from the epilogue
to the scenes which had unfurled.
Had my act have been less good,
or I had admitted what I should,
you would have recognised
the uncertainty of my mind.
Had I been a lesser fool,
or you had known my rules,
those partings might have been a softer kind.
How can I explain
that amidst all of the pain
and denials of the fact of human love
was an uncertain,
selfish man,
stumbling,
as any can,
whose self deceit
had grown around him like a glove.
Ah, but the memories still burn on,
of you,

and of all the ones,
reminders of regrets I have in life.
I who hurt you so,
who drove you all to go,
was the one who suffered most amidst the strife.
Had the lights had a lesser force,
or I'd followed a different course,
our stories may never have reached an end.
But,
there is still no guarantee,
that if another chance came to me,
I would play the part
as you all would recommend.

An Image Of Grace.

The wind swept
the tears
my lady wept
for me
across the sea.
Salt tears sting
my face
and bring
a vision to tease,
which my mind did seize.
An image of the grace
that haunts her face
is drawn to me,
here,
across the sea.
Sadness now
lines my brow
as love wanes
for my Lady Rain.
I hope she learns
I will not return
and does not wait
too long,
singing her sorrow's song,
for me to confer
once more,
my love upon her.

Gentle and Free.

A long time has passed,
little time before you go,
you came with the rain
and stayed through the snow.
You sat in the square,
for all there to see,
singing those sad songs,
so gentle and free.

Writing a song
for me to sing for you,
teaching that love
should be tender and true.
I remember you crying,
clinging to me,
before singing those sad songs,
so gentle and free.

You wanted to stay here
but melted away like the snow,
following the wind
wherever it blows.
Hearing your voice,
blown hauntingly to me,
singing those sad songs,
so gentle and free.

The words of your songs
recall memories undead,
the way that they left
so many questions unsaid.
Now all that remains
is the music you'd weave,
singing your sad songs,
so gentle and free.

On A Canadian Beach.

Time has tiptoed by me
I can only recall your face,
and the sound of the Pacific Ocean waves
breaking on that place.
You smiled when first I saw you,
as I passed you on the beach
your smile as I returned,
suggested you were within reach.
Seated together on a tree trunk
the sea had washed ashore;
you said,
'I wanted you to join me
when you passed me by before.'
You asked where I came from,
I simply answered,
'England'.
You told me you were a native
of this Canadian land.
Talking, then laughing together
our early awkwardness eased,
wandering along the shoreline,
walking where we pleased.
As we became lesser strangers
I slipped my hand in yours,
then you slid your arm around me
as we followed a lover's course.
Slowly daylight lessened
with a chill night,

pressing round,
so we snuggled down together
in your blanket on the ground.
Our talking steadily lessened,
the tension within us grew
to the point where we were desperate
to see that first kiss through.
As our lips first brushed together
the tension was resolved,
youth no longer restrained us
initial shyness was dissolved.
We spent some time just kissing,
learning a little more,
we felt the time approaching
for opening the lover's door.
It was a tremulous hand
I slipped inside your dress,
but you were just as willing
as your body against me pressed.
With only minor fumbles
we removed each other's clothes,
our nakedness we pressed together
to feel how passion flows.
We explored each other's body
with the quickness of the young,
before fusing together,
our own act of union.
Making love in inexperienced frenzy

our finale came too soon,
oh but that ecstasy,
I still recall,
here, in my lonely writing room.
As our passion was consumed,
the moon began to rise,
all remains of the word 'child'
had been eclipsed from our eyes.
Then we slept together
in your blanket on the ground,
until the Sun that rose next morning,
two older people found.
When the Sun was firmly risen
we went our separate ways,
but though your memory fades a little
I will remember you
always.

It was on Qualicum beach
we played our lover's game
and though I still recall your face,
I no longer recall your name.

Tomorrow, My Love Goddess.

Sat with the drunks,
alongside boozed up punks,
I asked for some room for my sorrow.
Then, drinking down the gin,
glasses full, ice cubes melting,
I left with a girl named Tomorrow.
    So I took the love that I stole from my Jewess,
    to give, next day, to my love seeking Goddess.

The morning sun scorched my eyes
as it lit up my well used lies,
recalling my words so profound.
Then a movement on the bed,
where, last night, those lines I'd said,
showed me Tomorrow had come around.
    I'd taken the love I'd stolen from my Jewess
    and given it, last night, to my love seeking
Goddess.

Tonight, trawling the bars,
for another wannabe film star,
 with whose body I'll stay.
Then, once more as morning comes
and my desire for her numbs,
she'll be another tomorrow that faded to Yesterday.
    So I'll take the love I've stolen from this Goddess,
    and give it Tomorrow, my love seeking Jewess.

Oh, Imaginary Mouth.

Oh, imaginary mouth,
gentle to touch,
soft red lips that promise much.
Oh tender tongue,
the brush of which
would enslave my soul as though bewitched.
Oh, imaginary breasts,
small and firm,
in passion thy very skin would burn;
stiff and taut as passion flows,
the press of which would make me grow.
Oh, imaginary thighs,
how wouldst thee compress
when my manhood into thee I press.
I would rise and fall and rise
until our passion's heat subsides.

Oh, imaginary body,
you I have known,
imaginary needs in you I have sown.
I've also been forced to feel the heartbreak
of the imaginary love our passion did make.

Diary Of A Letter.

Sunday.

Waiting for your letter,
forgetting there was no post.
Cursing, cursing the postman
before enjoying my Sunday roast.

Monday.

Out of bed quite early,
waiting for the postman to arrive.
He seemed so long in coming,
I looked for him
from the end of the drive.
Even then, the letters he delivered
were not addressed to me,
just a couple of bills,
an airmail, from overseas.

Tuesday.

No postman came to call.
I awaited him in vain,
for hours I stood there staring,
apparently it rained.

I wondered why you hadn't written,
wondered where you had been,
who had you been with,
what places had you seen?

Wednesday.

I overslept,
letters piled upon the floor,
still not one from you, though
the only sound, a slamming door.

Thursday.

A postcard
addressed to me by name,
not from you though,
but
about football,
I had a game.

Friday.

My nerves stretched taut,
up with the dawn,
postman late in arriving
waiting half the morn.

When he did wander up,
he proffered up one letter,
not from you but another friend,
still,
I felt a little better.

Saturday.

Still no letter,
by now I was resigned,
wondering, "What are you doing?"
A frown,
my forehead lined,
wondering
did you await me,
as I awaited you,
cursing me in turn,
I suppose I could
always write to you.

I Wondered At My Lack Of Ties.

Train departs the station,
dragging my life away,
knowing you'd not return
to me any day.
I wondered if you knew you'd lied,
wondered at the speed at which I'd died.
My forsaken heart cried out
to all those who would hear,
my red rimmed eyes burned
from the trickle of a tear.

A depth of hopelessness remained
as the year passed through its seasons.
I had no answers to the questions
or understandable reasons.
I wondered as I heard my sigh,
wondered that I still asked 'why?'
I no longer hear as people
speak their words to me,
nor do I look with their eyes
or see the things they see.

I share no close relationships
with people anymore,
just a flash of remembrance
of a slammed carriage door.
I wondered at my lack of ties,
wondered at my sad goodbyes.

Sometimes hating the memories
which remain behind of you,
always hating the nothingness
which follows on them too.

Scars, white in winter,
have not healed yet,
I no longer take a carriage,
though my wounds open in the wet.
I wondered that my mind still tried,
wondered that my heart still cried.
The madness is my own mind,
the medicine to make me sane,
left that now deserted station
in a one way ticket train.

I wondered at my lack of ties,
wondered at my sad goodbyes.

I wondered that my mind still tried,
wondered that my heart still tried.

I wondered as I heard my sigh,
wondered that I still asked, 'Why?'.

I wondered at the ease with which I died,
wondered if you knew you lied.

Section 4.

In most people's lives there are dark times, times when everything seems to conspire against you and the world seems an unlovely, stark place and your place within it uncertain. Such times can play upon your psyche and destroy your self confidence and if you have a mind set that can be drawn towards the dark, like I do, then, often, thoughts can lead to a fascination with the idea of death, natural or self inflicted, not just on my part, but also in friends that I have known. For many people the world we live in is a cold and lonely place and the way Society can appear to indiscriminately ignore the individual and their inner turmoil only exacerbates people's sense of isolation and dislocation.

Lost Battle.

My time is nearly over,
drawing to its close,
without a worthy memory;
so who cares,
or even knows.
Who cares about my sadness
or knows about my grief;
the loss of innocence
to experience,
that eternal thief.
Remembered aspirations
so long ago they died,
when events conspired together,
they were so cruelly crucified.
Shattered in the backlash,
of a fierce and bitter hate,
that twisted rite of passage,
the cynicism of fate.
A myriad of poisons
suffusing through the world,
bottled in camouflage colours,
confusion at me hurled.
Life,
which had seemed so simple,
now insinuated compromise,
my first defeat suffered,

I, too naïve to realise.
The trap was sprung so sweetly,
the poisons were the bait,
a choice of lesser evils
was the compromise debate.
All choices were irrelevant,
the end remained the same,
an illusion of battles won
in Society's game.
Hindsight makes it easy
to recognise how its cloying web
had trapped me within the tendrils
of Society's living death.
Now the spider is growing hungry
for this piece of poisoned meat,
no strength left to struggle,
resigned to my defeat.
Oh the weariness of living
with emptiness of hope,
a permanent solution
read my final horoscope.
Just another lonely statistic
Society has spurned,
living in isolation
until,
wolf-like,
I turned

to bare my fangs
in a suicidal fight,
crying my defiance
in the dusk of dying light.
Darkness closes round me,
heartbeat is stilled,
but my death did have some glory
which is all I could have willed.

Decision.

Greyness played before her morbid eyes,
eroding thoughts of life
as wave after wave of sensuous
nothingness
grasped at her.
Tendrils of lingered memories;
sadness,
hopelessness,
clung.

Far off,
yet half acknowledged,
a thought lies,
semi-dormant,
waiting beyond consciousness,
insidiously seeking admittance,
reaching upward toward decision,
a mind,
is greyer in its dying light.

Heartbeat,
steady,
mortal,
gives life
but a thought strives,
reaches consciousness.
Suicidal,
immortal.

Decision.
A rising tide of darkness,
grey to black,
choking, choked.
Heartbeat stopped,
drowned.
Convinced belief,
life is ended.
Is it?

Section 5.

Like most people I have often been hit by apparent vagabond thoughts that appear to come out of nowhere. What causes them to suddenly appear and infiltrate the mind is, and hopefully, will probably always be a mystery. These thoughts, without apparent origin, have often formed the basis for a subsequent poem. Sometimes, on occasion, poems have arrived virtually ready written in the mind and only little additional material or reworking is needed. The stimulus for such poems remains an enigma.

A Solitary Man Is All There Is.

Desolate calls echo within the air,
as, far above
the ravines and peaks
of mountainous oceans,
an albatross lies motionless upon the air.

Silence,
broken only by echoes of people
crying to their gods.

Forlorn remorse and dying atonement
echo emptily throughout the palaces of their gods,
but an Albatross is all there is.
Listening.

Isolation,
(a lost child) calls to me
to keep it solitary company,
but,
desolate calls of an Albatross also whisper to me,
(alone)
upon this mountain peak
a man sits motionless within the air,
searching for signs of his god
(alone).

Silence,
broken only by echoes
of people crying for their gods,
but,
a solitary man is all there is.
Listening.

*(Thanks to Pinkfloyd for supplying the initial
inspiration.)*

Watching the Stars Circle.

'Come dance with me',
the painted lady sang,
whilst the uncertain tourist,
stared
at the Navaho brave standing guard
over the pyre of his ancestor.

Ragged poles shrouded in blankets
woven wool and love;
consumed by fire,
scattered by the breeze,
ashes to ashes,
dust to dust.

The dead walk a pathway
strewn with embers,
and Navaho consciousness.
Sacred spirit ancestors,
real, unreal,
seen, unseen.

So,
watch the heathen dance.
drumming and chanting,
shuffling and hopping,
in, out of focus.
Mist reflects in red eyes,

as sparks fall from living flesh,
and a rite of passage
consumes the dead.

Stars circle in their
silver/black infinity.
Navaho warrior
infused with sacred spirits.

Uncertain and disturbed,
a white man watches the 'entertainment',
whilst the Painted lady hovers,
anticipating a chance of profit
as the night burns slowly by.

Sorrow's Sign.

Taking time
to interpret the sign
pointing to sorrow
consuming tomorrow.
A sudden sound
turned me around,
Old Voice declared,
'West,
that way is best.'
Quiet Voice whispered,
'East
is where you'll find peace.'

Closing my ears,
catching at my fears,
calling on instinct,
which said
'North',
so indistinct.
Turning that way,
clamorous voices crying,
'Stay.'
Hurrying along,
as the wind
whispered its song.

Sudden,
dark and black,
the malevolent air
appeared to crack.
Looking back
At the sign
Burned and black,
my choice confirmed.
However indistinct
follow your instinct.

It's Hard To Be Human.

It's hard to be human,
easier to be plastic,
first,
coat your skin
with a product called 'Tan-Fastic'.
It seems to bring no problems,
your tan looks really good,
but after years of use
you find
you have plastic blood.

When you take some exercise
and the hot sun is shining,
buy yourself a 'soft' drink,
give your stomach
a plastic lining.
Drink it standing up
or perched upon a fence,
a brand new plastic stomach
costs more than a few pence.

If dental care is forgotten,
they give you plastic teeth,
almost like the real thing,
but,
oft times,
you come to grief.
They're loose,

won't stay in,
how to fix them,
you haven't got a clue,
go to your nearest chemist
they'll sell you plastic glue.

Should you lose an arm (or two)
and need another one,
the NHS will help you
fit another one (or two) on.
So too for hands
or legs,
not to mention feet,
everything now replaceable,
limblessness defeated.

Organs no longer singular,
our heart, our lungs, our veins,
replaced with the cut of a scalpel,
are our doctors all quite sane?
for now all that's human
is our quintessential brain,
the rest of our bodies turned into
Cyborgs,
brains in a plastic frame.

Automatic Love.

I watched you take your arm off
and throw it on the pyre,
I saw it slowly melt there
leaving the skeletal wire.

I watched as you took your breasts off,
throw them with your arm,
the stench of burnt rubber
filled me with alarm.

I watched you take your legs off,
after undoing all the bolts,
I'd fallen in love with a robot,
I said it was all your fault.

Helping take your head off,
with a feeling of disgust,
but even after all these years
there is still no sign of rust.

Making a pilgrimage to where I'd met you,
I picked out another woman there,
making sure she was a robot too,
an automatic love we'll share.

Collection.

I feel something
calling,
within the galactic haze.
Falling,
sink beneath the waves.
Downward,
circle,
spiral round,
Outward,
toward the siren sound.

My body,
appendage drowning,
voice
belonging to no-one,
delicately tests
the caverns of my mind.
Vague impression
of the vastness of time.
Its swells,
depressions,
an ever flowing tide,
eternally ebbing,
cascading to either side.
Aeons of thought,
throbbing,

pulsating in my mind,
recognised
as the genius of time.
Surprised,
mingle slowly,
enter the matrix,
feeling somehow lowly,
though every thought fits.
Become one more feature
in this multi-faceted brain,
this galactic creature
evolving through constant change.

Section 6.

I am not sure whether I am an atheist or an agnostic; I do not accept that our lives are preordained or that there is nothing we can do to determine our future. I certainly do not believe in an omniscient being or creator who judges us or supplies our moral and social codes. Having said all of that, some form of religious or spiritual questions emerge in quite a few of my poems, as the following examples demonstrate.

Gods Need Atheists.

Oft times I have had a thought
and it becomes reality,
is brought into existence.
Does this make me god?
But I can't be a god
for I am an atheist.
I would not care to be a God,
living in isolation,
knowing everything
and believing everyone else
to be inferior.
Believers see their Gods as superior,

whose word is law,
unchallenged,
but,
with whom do gods debate
throughout the boredom of infinity.
Gods need atheists,
who else would treat them as equals.
They are the only beings
that gods can dispute
on equal terms with.

If so,
we could spend
the aeons in contention,
on our own doctrine we would insist,
yet, if I conversed with a god
how could I remain an atheist.
If gods and atheists are equal,
would that make me
a God,
or would God,
simply be human?

What Did You Mean To Say?

What did you really mean,
that day
looking at me,
that way
and telling me that you loved me;
before leaving with the twenty-third lover
you'd had since we'd known each other.

What did you really mean,
that day,
looking at me,
that way,
telling me that Jesus committed the greatest sin,
that without him, there would be no reason for the
wars his fanatics begin

What did you really mean,
that day,
looking at me,
that way,
and stating that I was a liar
for swearing I loved you,
when I was aiming for something higher.

What did you really mean,
that day,
looking at me,

that way,
before concluding,
with a voice so cold and level,
that your observations
had led you to believe that
Jesus was, without doubt, the Devil.

What did you really mean,
that day,
looking at me,
that way,
before telling me,
"I'm leaving you, Jesus,
because the war against love by your fanatics
has caused your devil to come between us".

Journey.

Dante waits impatiently,
the inferno at his rear,
yet who is he that I succumb
to burning fear.
Dante now is smiling,
as closer in I creep,
the booking clerk proffers
a ticket for me to keep.

My life is now the journey,
the heat is on this time.
Passing within those borders,
fear stultifies my mind.
Gabriel is pointing,
showing me 'the way'.
I never realised,
such forces he held at bay.
Lucifer,
standing close beside him,
fire burning within his eyes.

Two wraiths
stand waiting,
their task to be my guides.
The essence of good or evil
coalescing within their fire.
Their challenge
high and fearsome,

a potential funeral pyre.
My judge,
torture in his voice,
stood there before me,
intoned there was a judgement choice,
for crimes with which I was charged.

A year,
plus one day
to wander,
to suffer with the rest,
for a hope so slim and slender,
to pass the final test.
A year to wander
the inferno,
a day before his court,
a year seeking resolution
to that paralysing thought.

Mist draws around me,
wraiths beckon me away,
a journey through sadness and torture
for one year,
until,

Judgement Day.

Section 7.

The following poem was one of those that although the various sections do not appear related, the poem actually came to me all in one piece and almost seemed to write itself.

If Why Were A Vision.

Why do I write of the Sun and the Moon
in a poem that has them dying too soon?
Why is mankind portrayed in a way
that leads inevitably to its own decay?
Why are the stars left shining supreme
in a black, velvet night so darkly serene?
Why do I cry in helpless remorse
as the needle leads me again
on its visionary course?

What is this vision,
what do you see,
whose is this future
you're recounting for me?

Your body, hanging limp on a cross,
is naked to the voyeuristic air,
the words of the disciple

as he interprets his incredulous stare,
"Oh my god, you are a woman
that we have broken down."
Bloodied side, a spear thrust wound,
bloodied face beneath a thorny crown.
Why are you forsaken, oh Christ,
you are reduced in size,
merely a pair of up-thrust breasts,
a pair of rhythmic thighs.
Who'll follow a woman messiah,
you lead, we'll hesitate,
women envy your attraction,
men just want to copulate.
So hang there on that cross,
our poverty revealed,
call out to your father
of the pain your body feels.

What is this vision,
what do you see,
whose is this future
you're recounting for me?

Call out the Albatross
for the mariner to shoot,
an act of history
the gods won't refute.
Remember Neptune,
the bones in your depths
don't all belong to you.

Many are the bones of those murdered
for ignoring the mariner's curfew.
Beware Albatross
your death is at stake,
whilst the gods view your history
as a philosophical debate.
Remember Poseidon, the powers of gods
are delivered without justice or contempt
for mortal men, who pray
that the rising tides relent.
Sink now Albatross,
the gods have declared
that the mariner's shot
is how history fared.
Oh Neptune, Poseidon,
gods in debate,
why allow such a motion,
to legislate
that Death's companion,
be the bird of the ocean.

What is your vision,
what do you see,
whose is this future
you're recounting for me?

You sing of your love and of creation
but my seed you refuse in silent negation,
your songs reach a climax,
as did you,

but for my orgasm
I'd like to review
the past, present,
the depths of your mind
and why you refuse me
time after time?
Take this, my body,
an object to love,
wrap my penis inside you,
just like a glove,
let me commit my seed
to your womb
where all,
but one,
would be entombed.
But time now approaches to force my way in,
commit forever that cardinal sin,
for you are Mary,
my woman, my wife,
I am Joseph,
castrated by life.

What is this vision,
what do you see,
whose is this future
you're recounting for me?

Dancing so close
in a discothèque bar,
you felt my manhood

as a stiffened bar.
Giggling in my ear,
we made to resume
our place at the table
in the dark of the room.
One arm I put around you
the other I slipped
up to your thighs,
your knickers I gripped.
Finishing your vodka,
giggling some more,
we left for my room
where behind locked doors,
I was The Man
spurred on by your cries,
you were The Woman
who opened her thighs.
I collapsed in expiration
augmented by drink,
you rushed from the bed
to vomit in the sink.
We parted next morning,
both alone again,
now all that's between us
is the gently falling rain.

What was this vision,
what did you see,
whose was the future
you recounted for me?

Thanks to everyone who has been part of my life
and who has helped shape my experiences.

Special thanks to all at White Peak Writers for their
encouragement and support.

25671966R00038

Printed in Poland
by Amazon Fulfillment
Poland Sp. z o.o., Wrocław